For Mum and Dad—I. B.

First published by Candlewick Press

C P

CANDLEWICK PRESS
2067 MASSACHUSETTS AVENUE
CAMBRIDGE MA 02140

ISBN 0-590-99283-X

Text copyright © 1996 by Sam McBratney.
Illustrations copyright © 1996 by Ivan Bates.
All rights reserved. Published by Scholastic Inc.,
555 Broadway, New York, NY 10012, by arrangement with
Candlewick Press.

12 11 10 9 8 7 6 5 4   7 8 9/9 0 1/0

Printed in the U.S.A.   08

First Scholastic printing, October 1996

This book was typeset in Veronan Bold.
The pictures were done in crayon pencil.

THE DARK
AT THE **TOP** OF
THE STAIRS

Sam McBratney

illustrated by Ivan Bates

CANDLEWICK PRESS
CAMBRIDGE, MASSACHUSETTS

There was once a wise old mouse who lived with his young mice in the corner of a cellar.

Every day the old mouse liked to do something interesting with his young mice.

"What should we do tomorrow?" he said one bedtime, for the young mice were getting ready to sleep and he wanted them to look forward to the morning.

"I would like to see the dark at the top of the stairs," said a young mouse whose name was Cob.

"Me too," said his sister Hazel, snuggling into the warmth. "I want to see the dark at the top of the stairs."

"And so do I," said little Berry-Berry, the youngest of the three. "We've never been to the top of the big dark stairs where the monster lives."

The old mouse thought for a while. It was true that he had not taken his young mice up the cellar stairs.

Then he said, "What about a walk
to the acorn tree in the garden?

Or a visit to your cousins in the
cornfield? We could even have
a swing on the seedheads
of the long grass."

"No," said Cob. "We want to see the dark at the top of the stairs."

"Or we'll climb up there on our own," said Hazel.

"And see the monster by ourselves!" cried little Berry-Berry.

The old mouse nodded as he made his young mice comfortable in their bed.

"Very well then, we will go there in the morning," he said.

He spoke as if he knew that sooner or later all young mice will try to see the dark at the top of the stairs.

In the morning, as
early sunshine lit up
the cobwebs in the
corners of the cellar
windows, they set out
on their journey.

"Let's not talk about the monster," whispered Cob on the third step up.

"I won't mention it if you don't mention it," whispered Hazel.

"I won't talk about the monster either," laughed little Berry-Berry, who hadn't learned how to whisper yet.

After seven steps, they stopped once more. There was excitement in their eyes, and the young mice hardly dared to look up, for they were closer now than they had ever been to the dark at the top of the stairs.

"I wonder if it's really, really real?" whispered Cob.

"You said you wouldn't talk about it," whispered Hazel.

"I hope the monster knows we're coming!" cried little Berry-Berry.

On the tenth step up, only two from the top, they paused once more. Hazel turned to the old mouse and whispered, "What is the monster like? Is it the most terrible thing anyone has ever seen?"

"We don't have far to go now," the old mouse said, and climbed the last two steps. After him came Hazel and Cob and finally little Berry-Berry, who said, "I don't see any monster at the top of the stairs."

Then something
happened.
 The young mice
crept into a crack
of light . . .

They saw a monster shadow move
toward them as smoothly as a cloud,
and something breathed out softly
one strange word:

M E O W

The young mice did
not wait to say goodbye.
With wildly beating
hearts they went . . .

and tumble-thump

all the way to the bottom of the stairs, where they landed in a wriggle and a heap before making a dash for warm, safe, wonderful home.

At the end of the day the old mouse came to ask his young mice what they would like to do tomorrow.

"I would like to go to the acorn tree," said Cob.

"I would like to visit our cousins in the cornfield," said Hazel.

"I would like to swing backward and forward on the long grass!" said little Berry-Berry.

But none of them mentioned the dark at the top of the stairs.